MIRACLE M

JOHN HENDRIX

ABRAMS BOOKS FOR YOUNG READERS

NEW YORK

Ages ago, in a dry and dusty land, the people were in need.

The land was a sick place, in need of healing.
The land was a blind place, in need of sight.
The land was a thirsty place, in need of water . . .

. . . the kind of living water that would last forever.

On a day that didn't seem at all unusual, there came an unusual Man. He looked like any other man, but he was like none who had ever lived before. This Man was God's son. When he spoke, his words made things happen. His words came . . .

The Man found a group of hungry fishermen,
frustrated with their empty nets.
The Man said,

CAST YOUR NETS ON THE OTHER SIDE OF THE BOAT!

A fisherman named Simon
(who was later called Peter)
reluctantly obeyed.
His net came up bursting
with fish!

The fishermen were amazed.
The Man said,

FOLLOW ME
AND YOU'LL CATCH FISH OF A DIFFERENT KIND.

The fishermen followed the Man. They traveled to a town. As they walked, a leper came alongside them. The fishermen kept their distance, afraid of the leper's disease. But not the Man! Instead, he touched the leper on the face and tenderly put his arm around the sick man's shoulders. The leper knelt and said, "I know you can cleanse me, if you are willing."

The Man was still for a moment, then said,

I AM.
BE CLEAN.

The leper (who now could be called by some other name) forever lost his leprosy.
The astonished fishermen knew this Man was not like them.
This man was a Miracle Man.

A large crowd soon gathered to see the Miracle Man.

The friends of a boy who was paralyzed hoped to get him
to the Miracle Man, but the crowd was just too large. So
the friends made a plan. Pulling back the tiles on the roof
of the house where the Miracle Man was speaking, they
lowered the boy down on a mat, right in front of everyone!
When the Man saw their faith, he said to the boy,

FRIEND, I AM GOD'S SON SENT TO HEAL AND FORGIVE...

Not everyone liked the miracles, or the Miracle Man. There were some in the crowd with fancy clothes who taunted him.

you claim to be GOD's very SON? Are you a magician or just a LiaR?

The Miracle Man stood quietly and then said to the boy,

FRiEND, I say

The boy stood up, gingerly at first
. . . and then ran right past the
taunters in their fancy clothes!

Those men were powerful,
and now they were angry.
They hated how much the
people loved the Miracle
Man. They knew he
was trouble.

One evening, the Man told Peter to find a boat. He said there was work to be done on the other side of the sea.

As the tiny boat set out, the waves began to grow. Soon a great squall was breaking high over the deck. These fishermen were very good sailors, but the storm terrified them.

The wind and rain raged all around, but the Miracle Man was sleeping! Peter cried out,

DON'T YOU CARE IF WE DIE?

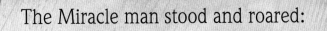

The Miracle man stood and roared:

And the storm ended in an instant.

The Man looked at the trembling fishermen and said,

I AM THE SON OF THE LIVING GOD WHO MADE THE WATER AND THE WINDS.

DID YOU FORGET WHO WAS IN YOUR BOAT?

The Man traveled from one dusty town to another. The fishermen (whom he called the twelve disciples) always followed behind. He covered the eyes of the blind with his hands, and they could see. The sick touched his robe and were made well.

I NEED TO BE ALONE FOR A TIME.

But the endless crowds made the Man tired. One night, he told the disciples,

The disciples sat around their small fire together . . . and worried.

One doubtful disciple said,

In the morning, the disciples woke up to a delicious smell. The Miracle Man had returned and was cooking them fish. Handing them breakfast, he said,

IT is TIME TO RETURN. THERE ARE MANY WHO NEED WAITING TO

Indeed, the Man found a gigantic crowd waiting for him nearby. He stayed and spoke among them all day, until it was very late. Finally, one of the disciples said,

WE CAN NEVER FEED ALL THESE PEOPLE! YOU SHOULD SEND THEM AWAY SO THEY CAN FIND SOMETHING TO EAT.

The Man saw a girl with a small basket of bread and fish. "Child," the Man said, "would you give up your basket if it could feed everyone here?"

Peter laughed and said,

HOW ARE FIVE LOAVES AND TWO FISH GOING TO FEED SO MANY?

The child handed her basket to the Miracle Man. The Man gave thanks and broke the loaves and fish, giving some to each disciple to pass out to the crowd. He kept breaking and breaking and breaking . . . and filled every mouth with bread and fish.

HOW IS THIS POSSIBLE?

The Miracle Man said, "I am the bread of life."

WITH ME THERE IS ABUNDANCE FOREVER.

The Man was again tired and needed rest. So he sent the disciples on ahead of him to cross the sea once more, this time alone. As the hours drifted by and the wind blew cold, the disciples felt abandoned and scared.

Then they saw a distant figure coming toward them. He was striding across the waves! The disciples cried out in fear,

A GHOST ON THE WATER!

A voice they recognized called back, "Take courage. It is I! Did you think I would leave you?"

Peter leapt out of the boat. His feet held firm on the
sea, just as if it were dry land. With his gaze fixed
on the Miracle Man, he walked on the water!
Then he looked down at his feet, amazed. And
he started to sink in the roiling water. "Help me!"
he cried out as his head went under.

Quickly taking his hand, the Man pulled
Peter up to the surface and said,

After their journey, the Man called his disciples together for a meal. He blessed the bread and wine and said, "It is time for me to leave you. I will be broken like this bread and poured out like this drink. One of you will betray me, and the flock will be scattered."

The disciples were astonished
and cried out in denial.
As the shouting grew, the
doubting disciple (called Judas)
fled from the table.

After dinner, as the disciples and the Miracle Man rested in an inky-dark garden, everything changed.

For a bag of silver coins, Judas had turned into a betrayer. He led the rich taunters and their soldiers to arrest the Man. These powerful people with their fancy clothes were tired of listening to everyone talk about the Miracle Man. They feared that the crowds would no longer listen to *them!* The taunters had decided it was time for the miracles to end.

Some disciples ran away, and some disciples fought. But the Man raised his hand and said to them,

To Judas he said, THIS IS YOUR HOUR, WHEN DARKNESS REIGNS.

The soldiers led the Miracle Man away, into the shadows.

The Miracle Man was sent to die.
The disciples (who just wanted to be called fishermen again)
were heartbroken.

But God's Son, Jesus, the Miracle Man,
had in store one last glorious miracle . . .

AUTHOR'S NOTE

This book is based on the life of Jesus, as found in the Bible, in the Gospels of Matthew, Mark, Luke, and John. *Miracle Man* is my own version of this story. Though based on the gospel narrative of his life and ministry, it should not be confused with the authority of the actual Biblical accounts. The words of Jesus and the disciples here are not direct quotations but my own interpretations of his life and teachings on Earth. These interpretations are not from the head of an academic but from the heart of a disciple.

The first reason I wanted to write and illustrate this story is that I am a follower of Jesus. At a very young age, I fell in love with the Miracle Man. To this day, merely reading his words in the simple clarity of the Gospel story can stir my soul. I vividly remember being drawn to the red ink of his words in my very first Bible. The stark black-and-white tones of the Scriptures were broken with that sudden incarnation of vibrant crimson! In many ways, the illustrated and illuminated text in this book is aspiring to be like that first Bible of mine, bringing his words into vivid life.

You may have heard about the life of Jesus many times before, but my hope is to share the familiar story with you in a new way. Perhaps the best way to experience the Easter story is to momentarily forget about the trappings of religion around it and see the man at the center. In my experience, the story changes when we think of the people who experienced Jesus in person during the time he walked among us. Those people didn't have a steepled church building or know anything about Christian theology. They simply met a man, some of them for only a brief moment, and they were changed forever.

Creating an illustrated book about the life of Christ is both a frightening challenge and a dream come true. As with all stories that have been told many, many times before, it is hard to avoid the familiar, well-worn paths. This is a particular challenge when visually depicting Jesus himself. In this book, I have aspired to render him as a man of his time and place and not as a construction of western idealism. Also, I stripped the story of some particulars in order to focus on the Miracle Man himself. There are very important characters who are not included in this story, for the sake of brevity. For example, Jesus had important interactions with Mary Magdalene and Martha and Mary of Bethany. In fact, women were the first people

to see the risen Jesus, but my narrative ends before this moment. Also, some characters are named, but many are not. These edits and omissions were not meant to obscure but rather to cast the familiar in a new light. I regret leaving anything out, but even the Gospel writer John notes this in John 21:25: "Now there are also many other things that Jesus did. Were every one of them to be written, I suppose that the world itself could not contain the books that would be written."

Despite being one of the oldest stories humankind has ever continually told, the story never grows tired to my ears. Jesus did not remain in the tomb on Easter morning . . . and the unbelievable story of God Himself on Earth walked out with him.

STORIES INCORPORATED INTO THIS BOOK

The stories are from the following versions of the Bible: English Standard Version (ESV),
New International Version (NIV), and New King James Version (NKJ).

The Calling of the Disciples and the
Miraculous Catch of Fish
Luke 5:1–11

The Healing of the Leper
Luke 5:12–15, Mark 1:40–45, and Matthew 8:1–4

The Healing of the Paralytic
Matthew 9:1–8 and Luke 5:17–26

Jesus Calms the Storm
Matthew 8:23–27 and John 8:22–25

The Healing of the Blind Man
John 9:1–12

The Feeding of the Five Thousand
Matthew 14:13–21 and John 6:1–15

Jesus Walks on Water
Matthew 14:22–36

The Last Supper
Matthew 26:17–30 and Luke 22:1–38

The Betrayal of Christ
John 18:1–14

The Crucifixion
Luke 23:26–43 and John 19:17–37

The Resurrection of Christ
John 20:1–18 and Luke 24:1–12

ABOUT THE ART: The illustrations were inspired by Biblical artwork from many different generations of visual storytellers, from Giotto
di Bondone to Albrecht Dürer. But many of those artists set their images in a European environment. Although *Miracle Man* is visually
metaphorical, the settings and locales have been anchored in the time and place of Jesus in the Middle East around the Sea of Galilee and
Jerusalem. Among the things I researched were what people looked like, what clothes they wore, how buildings—especially rooftops—
were constructed, and even if there were butterflies in the region!

 DEDICATED TO MY GRANDPARENTS, IN THE COMMUNION OF SAINTS
—DORIS, EARL, HAZEL, AND JOHN

SPECIAL THANKS TO PASTOR KURT LUTJENS AND PASTOR THURMAN WILLIAMS OF GRACE & PEACE
FELLOWSHIP IN ST. LOUIS, MISSOURI, FOR THEIR INSPIRATION AND ADVICE.

THE ILLUSTRATIONS IN THIS BOOK WERE MADE WITH PEN AND INK WITH FLUID ACRYLIC WASHES ON STRATHMORE BRISTOL VELLUM.

Library of Congress Cataloging-in-Publication Data

Hendrix, John, 1976– author, illustrator.
Miracle man : the story of Jesus / John Hendrix.
pages cm
Summary: "This picture book written and illustrated by John Hendrix focuses on the Biblical accounts of miracles performed by Jesus and concludes with the Crucifixion and the Resurrection.
There is a detailed author's note and a list of Biblical passages."—Provided by publisher.
Audience: Ages 5+
ISBN 978-1-4197-1899-1
1. Jesus Christ—Miracles—Juvenile literature. I. Title.
BT366.3.H46 2016
232.9'55—dc23
2015018202

Text and illustrations copyright © 2016 John Hendrix. Book design by John Hendrix and Chad W. Beckerman.

10 9 8 7 6 5 4 3 2 1

Abrams Books for Young Readers are available at special discounts when purchased in quantity for premiums and promotions as well as fundraising or educational use.
Special editions can also be created to specification. For details, contact specialsales@abramsbooks.com or the address below.

ABRAMS
THE ART OF BOOKS SINCE 1949
115 West 18th Street
New York, NY 10011
www.abramsbooks.com